Monster
CHRISTMAS

For Eddie, with love – G.A.

For my dear Uncle Alan,
who always loved Christmas – N.D.

ORCHARD BOOKS
First published in Great Britain in 2020 by The Watts Publishing Group

1 3 5 7 9 10 8 6 4 2

Text © Giles Andreae, 2020 • Illustrations © Nikki Dyson, 2020

ISBN 978 1 40835 762 0
Printed and bound in China

FSC
www.fsc.org
MIX
Paper from
responsible sources
FSC® C104740

Orchard Books
An imprint of Hachette Children's Group
Part of The Watts Publishing Group Limited
Carmelite House, 50 Victoria Embankment
London, EC4Y 0DZ

An Hachette UK Company
www.hachette.co.uk
www.hachettechildrens.co.uk

ORCHARD

Monster
CHRISTMAS

Giles Andreae

Nikki Dyson

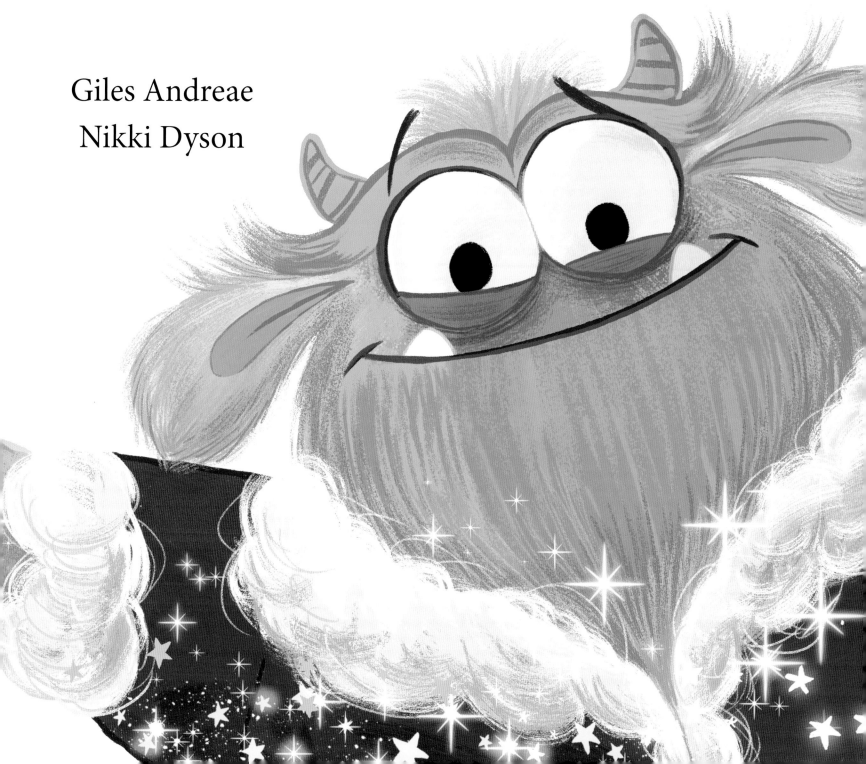

One evening, Father Christmas
Was relaxing by the fire.
"I'm getting rather old," he thought.
"Perhaps I should retire.

Heaving round those heavy sacks
Is more than I can take,
And my knees are getting creaky . . .
Yes, I **REALLY** need a break."

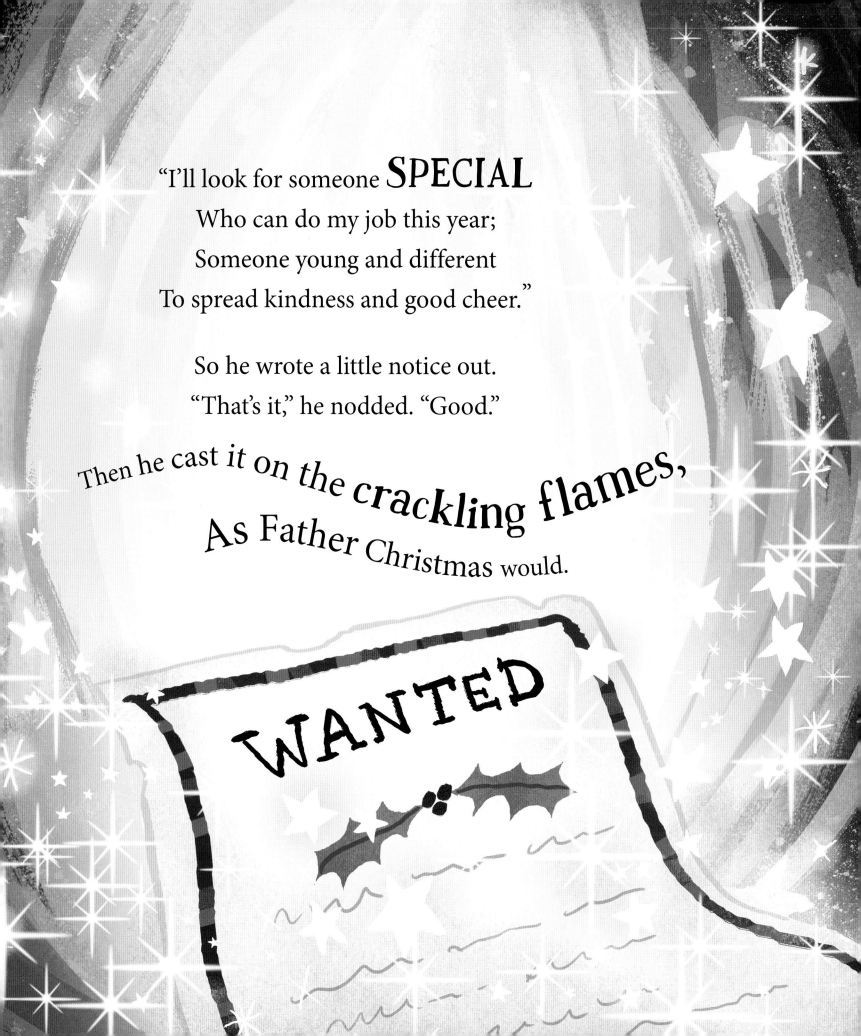

"I'll look for someone SPECIAL
Who can do my job this year;
Someone young and different
To spread kindness and good cheer."

So he wrote a little notice out.
"That's it," he nodded. "Good."

Then he cast it on the crackling flames,
As Father Christmas would.

WANTED

Far away in Monster Land,
A family ate their tea,
When the son said, "Listen, Mummy,
We've been talking, Dad and me.

I want to start to do those things
A grown-up monster should;
To stretch my wings, to see the world,
And maybe . . . do some good!"

Just when he'd finished speaking,
Something **drifted through the air**.
The little monster caught it,
And he read it then and there.

WANTED

"THAT'S IT!"
he said, "that's perfect!
Oh, I love you both.
Goodbye!"

Then he fetched his
favourite teddy
As his mummy
wiped her eye.

The monster trudged through sleet and snow.
His feet grew tired and sore.
But, finally, he stood
At Father Christmas's front door.

NORTH POLE

MONSTER LAND

"Welcome, friend!" the old man said,
"How wonderful you've come.
You're just the fellow for this job.
We're going to have such fun!"

The monster
found his workshop,
Where he trained
all night and day.

He **fed** and **groomed**
the reindeer,

And he **polished**
up the sleigh.

Until, at last, "It's time!"
Said Father Christmas,
with a grin.

"You're ready,
MONSTER
CHRISTMAS,
Yes, your job can now begin!"

Monster Christmas built a grotto
In a busy shopping mall,
And hung a sign outside that said,

You're WELCOME, ONE and ALL!

A mummy was just passing,
With her little boy in tow.
"There's Father Christmas! Look!" she said.
"Let's go and say hello!"

The boy looked up. He stopped. He screamed.
"HELP, MUMMY! HELP!" he bleated.
"Father Christmas is a MONSTER ...

AND I'M GOING TO GET
EATED!"

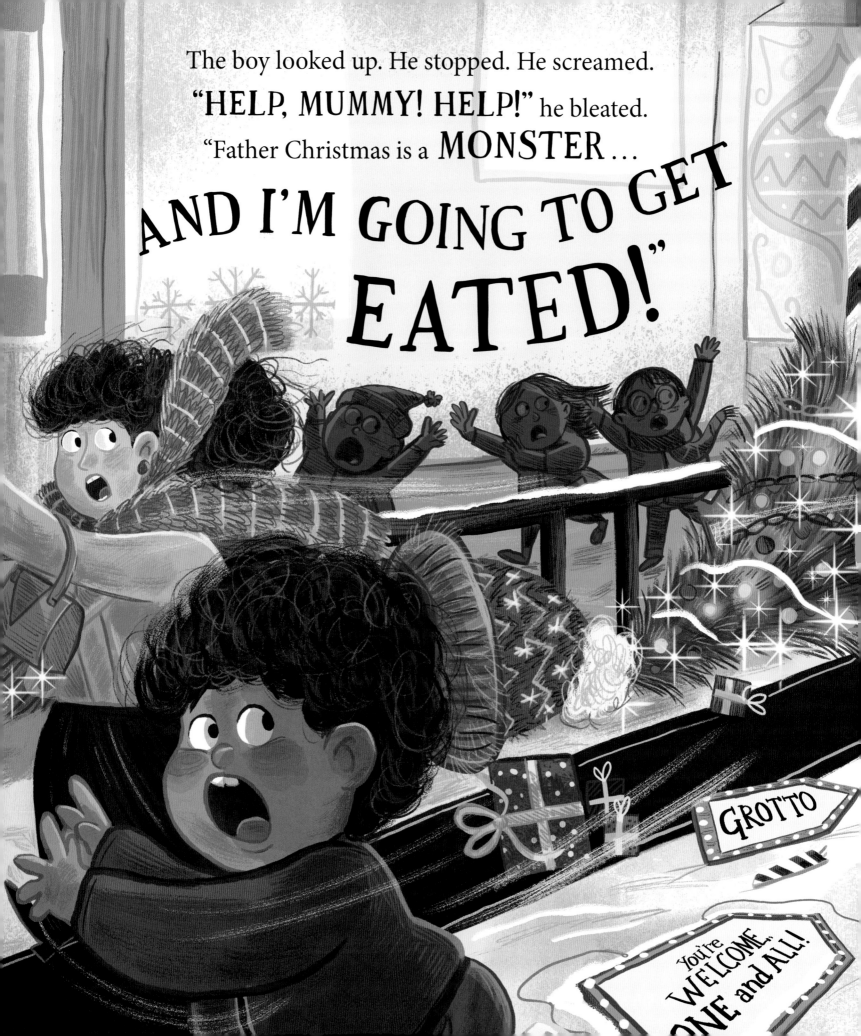

Everybody panicked,
And amidst the howls and shrieks
Monster Christmas stood alone,
Tears rolling down his cheeks.

"I know that I look different,
But whatever they may say,
They're going to love me soon," he sniffed.
"Tomorrow's Christmas Day!"

But news had spread from town to town:
No children would be spared,
And when the night began to fall,
The world was well prepared.

MONSTERS NOT WELCOME!

DOWN WITH THIS SORT OF THING!

NO MONSTERS!

Every window, every door,
In every home was locked.
And every single chimney
In the whole wide world was blocked.

GO AWAY!

And when poor
Monster Christmas
And his sleigh came flying by,
The people down below him
Shook their fists up at the sky.

"LET'S GO!"
his reindeer shouted.
We're done. That's it.
ENOUGH!

NO ONE wants to see you
And we're running out of puff!"

Inside an icy igloo,
On the far edge of the world,
Where the land becomes the ocean,
Lay a lonely little girl.

And as she slumbered softly,
All cosy, safe and sound,
A **MONSTER** tumbled through the roof,
And landed on the ground.

She didn't scream. She didn't run.
She knew he meant no harm.
Instead, she took him gently
And she held him in her arms.

"Wake up,
lovely monster,
And I'll be your
friend," she said.

Then she sung him songs
and kissed him,
As she softly stroked his head.

And slowly, very slowly,
As the moon lit up the sky,
Monster Christmas raised his head,
And opened up one eye.

"I don't know who you are," he said,
"But please don't be afraid.
You're the **kindest**,
sweetest creature
That this world has ever made."

Then he saw his sleigh and reindeer
Grazing happily outside.
"Would **YOU** like some presents?"
Said the monster, " . . . or a ride?

I've tried delivering these gifts,
But everyone's the same.
They just see what I look like,
Then they shout and call me names."

"I don't need any presents,"
Laughed the girl, "and anyway,
I've got just what I wished for now –
A FRIEND FOR CHRISTMAS DAY!

But let me come out with you.
I can help to make this right.
We'll let your reindeer rest for now,
Then ride when it gets light."

And sure enough, once they had slept,
At sunrise the next day,
Monster Christmas and his friend
Climbed back into that sleigh.

And very soon, the children,
Then the grown-ups came to see
That this monster was no different
To **them** … or **you** … or **me**.

What's more, he'd shown the world
That **ANYONE** can be your friend,
And that kindness is the only thing
That matters in … **THE END.**